For Sandra

Copyright © 1994 by Peter Utton
First American Edition 1995 published by Orchard Books
First published in Great Britain by ABC, All Books for Children, in 1994

Orchard Books
95 Madison Avenue
New York, NY 10016

Printed and bound in Hong Kong

10 9 8 7 6 5 4 3 2 1

Library of Congress Cataloging-in-Publication Data
Utton, Peter.
Jennifer's room / Peter Utton. – 1st American ed.
p. cm.
"First published in Great Britain by ABC, All Books for Children, in 1994"–T.p. verso.
Summary: Little by little the things in a young girl's room change from familiar to extraordinary, as her
chair becomes an elephant, her rug becomes a fish pond, and her desk becomes a castle.
ISBN 0-531-06842-0
[1. Imagination–Fiction.] I. Title.
PZ7.U73Je 1995
[E]–dc20   93-44482

JENNIFER'S ROOM

Peter Utton

Orchard Books
New York

Jennifer couldn't remember
exactly when things began
to change...

...but one moment her picture book
was balanced on her favorite chair...

and the next moment it was on the floor.
"Whoops!"

And one minute she was drawing a
picture of her best friend Alice . . .

but then the next moment she was
drawing a picture of an Allosaurus.
"Hmmm," Jennifer murmured.
And then her best blue pencil
shivered, turned green, and slithered
along the edge of her desk.

"Urrgh!" shouted Jennifer, and
she jumped into her favorite chair...

which barked politely and changed
into an old baggy . . .

. . . elephant!

And then, out of the corner of her eye, she saw her wallpaper change from small blue forget-me-nots into dark smudgy thunderclouds.

That's odd, thought Jennifer.
Then suddenly the wind roared . . .

. . . then stopped just as suddenly.
"Wow!" said Jennifer.

Then . . .

...her lamp grew into a beautiful tall tree, her bed stretched into a bridge to somewhere, and her rug rippled into a magical fish pond.

Her toy box became a pirates'
treasure chest and her desk
a small giant's castle. Only
teddy stayed the same.

Wonderful! thought Jennifer.

And she didn't mind a bit...

. . . because by this time
she was pretty wonderful herself.

"Whoopee!" cried Jennifer.
And she fluttered to the
top of the page.

Suddenly her mother called out.

Jennifer...
Dinner's ready!

"Coming, Mother!" she called.
And she landed with a bump.

And everything was
back to how it should be. . . .

Almost!